This fu
belongs to

Contents

Ladybird

Cover illustration by Spike Gerrell

A catalogue record for this book is available from the British Library

Published by Ladybird Books Ltd
27 Wrights Lane London W8 5TZ
A Penguin Company

2 4 6 8 10 9 7 5 3 1

by Clive Gifford
illustrated by Spike Gerrell

introducing the **ff** and **st**
letter groups, as in sniff and best

Big Bad Wolf scared
the storekeeper stiff.

"I'll huff and I'll puff,
then I'll steal all your stuff,"
he said.

But Sheriff Showoff was riding past.

"I'm the best in the West.
I'm faster than all the rest,"
he said.

Big Bad Wolf just gave a sniff.

“I’ll huff and I’ll puff, then I’ll knock your block off,” he said.

There was a scuffle in the dust.

Wolf ran off...

leaving Sheriff Showoff
handcuffed, in just his vest.

by Clive Gifford

illustrated by Karl Richardson

introducing the **mp** **lp** and **nch**

sounds, as in jump, help and pinch

Up jumped Mr Crump!

"Help!" he yelped. "It's the Bogie Bunch! They've come to gulp us down for lunch!

“They will pinch us
and punch us!

They will crunch us and munch us!

“They will stamp on us,
stomp on us,

chop up and chomp on us!"

Mrs Crump put on the lamp.

"It's just Scamp and Plump,
you silly old lump!"

Mr Crump flumped back,
in a grump.

Handstand Andy and Bendy Wendy

by Richard Dungworth

illustrated by Becky Cole

introducing the **nd** and **fl** sounds, as in bend and flap

This is my friend Andy and his little sister Wendy.

The two of them, as you can see, are very, very bendy.

Wendy likes to spend the weekend doing flip-flap-flops,

end over end, again and again, then she flops down flat and stops.

Andy, on the other hand, likes handstands best of all.

On the bandstand,

in the grandstand,

or up against
a wall.

I'm sure that you would find it
odd to see us all out shopping,

Andy standing on his hands, and Wendy flip-flap-flopping.

phonics

Learn to read with Ladybird

phonics is one strand of Ladybird's **Learn to Read** range. It can be used alongside any other reading programme, and is an ideal way to support the reading work that your child is doing, or about to do, in school.

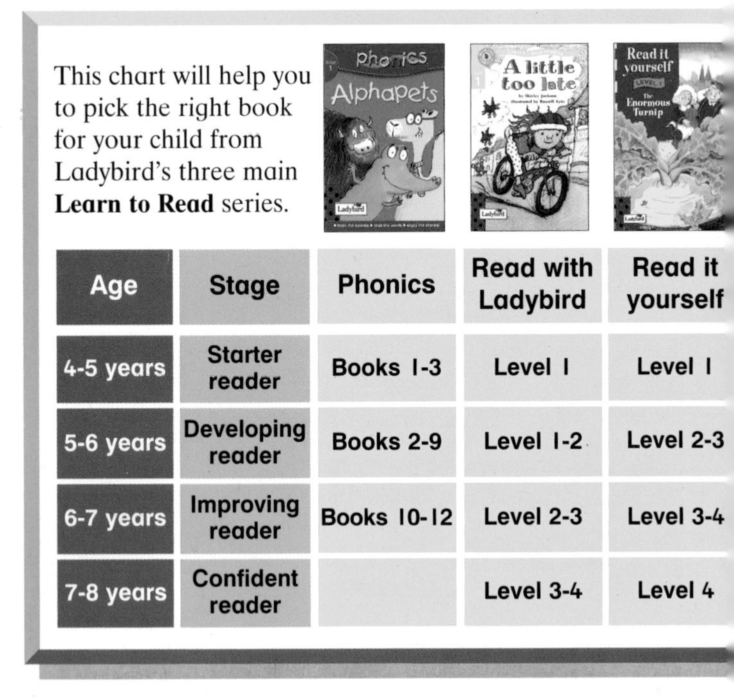

This chart will help you to pick the right book for your child from Ladybird's three main **Learn to Read** series.

Age	Stage	Phonics	Read with Ladybird	Read it yourself
4-5 years	Starter reader	Books 1-3	Level 1	Level 1
5-6 years	Developing reader	Books 2-9	Level 1-2	Level 2-3
6-7 years	Improving reader	Books 10-12	Level 2-3	Level 3-4
7-8 years	Confident reader		Level 3-4	Level 4

Ladybird has been a leading publisher of reading programmes for the last fifty years. phonics combines this experience with the latest research to provide a rapid route to reading success.

- Some common words, such as ‘would’, ‘said’ and even ‘the’, can’t be read by sounding out. Help your child practise recognising words like these so that she can read them on sight, as whole words.

Phonic fun

Playing word games is a fun way to build phonic skills. Write down a consonant blend and see how many words your child can think of beginning or ending with that blend. For extra fun, try making up silly sentences together, using some or all of the words.

Flo flung the flan flat on the floor, with a flop.

**The text applies equally to girls and boys, but the child is referred to as ‘she’ throughout to avoid the use of the clumsy ‘he/she’.*

Books in the phonics series

Book 1 Alphapets
Introduces the most common sound made by each letter, and the capital and small letter shapes.

Book 2 Splat cat
Simple words including the short vowel sounds a e and i as in cat, hen and pig.

Book 3 Hot fox
Simple words including the short vowel sounds o and u ; simple words including ch sh or th.

Book 4 Stunt Duck
Simple words including the common consonant combinations ck ll ss and ng.

Book 5 Sheriff Showoff
More words including common consonant blends: ff st mp lp nch nd and fl .

Book 6 Frank's frock
More words including common consonant blends: fr nk cl tr gr and nt.

Match the sounds gan

36 self-checking phonic gamecards. Great fun, and the id way to practise the spellings and introduced in the phonics stor